League of Assassins

Betrayal

Written by Mike and Longine S.
Edited by Julie Tarman

Copyright

Table of Contents

The Shadow Titan

Year 1520 of the Fourth Astra Reign

The rain fell for months in the region and the forests were thick and lush because of it. From deep within the canyons of the White Lions Mountain range, the war drums of the Sky Castle announced the movement of the Astra Knight army. The realm was deeply entrenched in a savage war between forces of the Light and forces of the Dark. The Astra King's grip on the realm slowly began to slip, for the Shadow spread down from the North and so the tension mounted. The High Mountain Road ran deep into the White Lions Mountains, and it acted as the only true route of transportation through the treacherous hills. Astra Knights were seen day and night as they patrolled and conducted security checks to protect the region from intruders, especially in such dangerous times. Often seen in the distances were their torches, and if those were not in sight, one only had to look hard for the bright gleam of their Astra Blades. Blades made from the hardest and most powerful element in the entire realm. Even through the darkest of shadows, Ether Glass would light the way.

A hooded figure emerged from the forest. He walked slowly and with purpose, as he followed the Astra Knights from a distance, eyeing them.

Stalking them, hunting them.

Each step sank into the Earth under his immense weight and when he stood tall, his height reached well over seven feet. A long black cape trailed behind him and rustled silently in the wind; it appeared to meld into the shadows, giving it the semblance that it was endless. Giant strides brought him closer and closer to the unsuspecting soldiers and yet they could not hear or sense him. He moved like a shadow, he was a shadow, seemingly catlike in his agility, and he found himself within arm's reach in a matter of seconds. From beneath his cloak, his hand emerged, in his palm hovered a black orb of energy that throbbed with the intensity of a dying star. In one motion he swept his arm across the backside of four Astra Knights and sent them flying into the forest like they were children's dolls. Before the other Knights realized what had happened, the man turned to them and drew his other hand out. As he did, the ball of black energy formed into a long jagged black blade, six feet in length that sliced through their armor and flesh, discerning no difference between the two. The Astra Knights crumpled into pieces, their wounds sizzled and smoked, and were charred black as night. The Shadow Titan smirked beneath his hood, and returned his hands beneath his cloak as he marched on down the road.

"Halt! Stop right there sir, show your face." Two armed Astra Knights stood determined a hundred yards away.

The Shadow Titan lowered his gaze, and moved on without looking up at them.

"Sir, you are trespassing on the land of the Astra King, ruler of the Sky Kingdom and the White Lions Mountain region. As an Astra Knight of the King's first regiment, I order you to stop where you are this instant."

The Shadow Titan stopped dead in his tracks and slowly raised his gaze. A deep guttural laugh emerged from beneath his hood. The Astra Knights drew their swords, baffled looks on their faces made it seem like they were unsure of what else they could do.

"Remove your hood or we will be forced to attack you sir, and we will not hold back if you continue to disobey our orders." The Astra Knight on the left stepped forward, and kept his sword pointed toward the Shadow Titan. His partner on the right stood behind him with a nervous look on his face.

The Shadow Titan stepped forward, now within striking distance of the two Knights. He turned his head and stared only at the Knight in the rear, as he ignored the knight directly in front of him. For a brief second a cloud of darkness fell over the Knight's eyes.

"Do not make another move, or I will be forced to—" The Knight's body dropped to the ground, blood sprayed from his neck and his head rolled down past the Shadow Titan's feet and settled onto the side of the road in a shallow mud puddle. The other Knight fell to his knees, a look of disbelief on his face, clutching his sword that dripped with his partner's blood. A look of horror on his face as he stared in shock at his blade, then slowly looked up at the Shadow Titan, who had remained perfectly still and silent as far as the Astra Knight could tell, this entire time.

"How?" was all he managed to sputter before the man of darkness leaped into the air, his Shadow Blade emerging from beneath his cloak.

All was silent as he moved in one motion to cleave off the head of the remaining Knight. The sizzle of skin and the dull thud of a head hitting the ground several yards away was the only noise to be made.

The Shadow Titan turned his head, and stared back into the forest for a moment, looking long and hard into the darkness. Slowly he turned back and continued his way up the road. The Sky Castle loomed large in the distance, another three days march without rest at least. The immense towers stood tall, even against the backdrop of the mountains, while the great wall that defended the castle wrapped around and into the mountainside, looming nearly a mile high and a quarter mile deep. The wall was made of impenetrable Ethereal Glass or Ether Glass for short, the substance so pure and true, that it could cut through even the darkest of evils. Like clockwork, every two thousand years, when the gravitational nexus of the Light Sun and the Dark Sun crossed paths; two asteroids met the Earth in nearly the same locations. One asteroid landed in the North, in an area known as the Shadow Kingdom. It was enshrouded at all times by deep black clouds and dark, sinister magic known to be used there. Across the realm, there was a decree issued by the Astra King, that these Dark Magic be deemed unnatural and therefore against the natural order. In retaliation, the Shadow King declared war, and unleashed his army on every corner of the realm.

Darkness fell and the rain persisted, yet the Shadow Titan trudged on relentlessly. In the distance he heard the sounds of men, yelling and laughing.

"Fools," he whispered to himself, his attention drawn toward the men. He moved quickly into the shadows of the edge of the forest that lined the road. Eventually, he saw the bright flames of the campfire that this troop of Astra Knights made for the night. He counted at least eight of them, fully armed.

"Salazar," a voice in his head called to him, for that was the Shadow Titan's name. Salazar knelt back into the shadows to listen for further instructions.

"Dispose of those men as discreetly as possible, there are more troops further on down the road and we need to draw as little attention to ourselves as possible."

"Understood." And just as quickly as it appeared the voice was gone, it left Salazar alone in the shadows as he listened intently to the laughter of the Knights, and the sounds of the rain that fell all around him. Salazar moved stealthily through the trees as he circled around the campsite to gain an advantage. Many of the soldiers would be drunk on ale, making it easier for him.

There was a rustle in the bushes behind Salazar, and he whipped around, reacting to the slight sound of a small branch cracking, but there was nobody there.

Salazar refocused on the task at hand, spotting an armed watchguard several yards off. He crouched down low and slipped through the bushes, and within seconds he laid the body of the guard down, throat agape and spewing blood, like a slaughtered animal. The rest of the Knights remained oblivious. Salazar held his hand up toward the group of Knights and before their eyes, their campfire roared to life, from a calm crackling red to a menacing and ominous black that gave off no light. The Knights were instantly sobered, reaching frantically for their swords and armor, but in the darkness it was chaos, and Salazar ran in wildly with two full Shadow Blades. The screams were bloodcurdling and guttural as one by one the Knights were eviscerated, even in the shadows, their blood sprayed violently across the forest, painting the trees a deep crimson. In a matter of moments, it was finished. Salazar sat down next to the fire and drained the last of the horn of ale. The smell of roasted boar drifted invitingly to him and he helped himself to a large helping of meat. The metallic stink of blood and entrails wafted in the air throughout the night, and while Salazar slept, birds, rodents and small foxes cautiously approached to feed on the corpses. On one occasion, Salazar awoke with a start, he scanned through the darkness, but again he saw nothing. Somewhere in the darkness, off in the distance, he made out the faint, yet unmistakable sound of a man running.

It was forty years since the last asteroids fell, and for forty years the realm warred over the precious materials that were harvested from them. This was the furthest that the Astra Kingdom was penetrated thus far, and Salazar was on the verge of reaching the crater. He knew that there would more than likely be another line of defense that he would need to overcome. He waited in the surrounding forest until darkness fell, but no Astra Knights approached the area for hours. Finally, just as Salazar was going to leave his perch, a troop of six armed Knights marched by carrying torches. He crouched in the shadows and listened to them as they passed.

"It's been forty fucking years since this thing has fallen and nobody has been within a hundred miles of here!" one of the Knights complained to the others.

"They are our orders and who are we to disobey them? Besides, it's more peaceful here than being sent out to a battle somewhere against Shadow Knights."

A murmur of agreement came from the troops as they stopped to rest. They unstrapped their belts and lay their weapons down on the ground. Even in the darkness with only the faint, flickering glow from the flames of the torches, their Ether Glass blades resonated brightly. The first Knight used his torch to light up a pipeful of tobakk leaf and he sat back and smoked it thoughtfully before he continued on his rant.

"Do any of you know when the last time a Shadow Knight or any other intruder was seen in these parts?" He continued when none of them replied, "Not since I've been an Astra Knight, that's for sure."

"I'll smoke to that, you can say the same for me," another Knight spoke up, spitting after he toked from his pipe.

The men smoked in silence after that, until their torches nearly burned out. Salazar remained hidden, patiently waiting for any other troops that might come along.

But none came.

Just beyond the clearing where the Knights sat, he could see the humming glow of the Great Crater where shards of Ether Glass still lay embedded in the earth and sparkled like stars across a midnight sky.

An older Knight spoke up then, and the troop all looked, listening with rapt attention. Judging from his voice he was the first that replied to the outspoken Knight.

"You lads better enjoy the quiet while you can; there is something sinister brewing in the North, you mark my words." He nodded with his head over toward a great divide in the mountains. Dark, billowing black clouds crested the skyline in the distance like smoke.

"Only something truly unnatural can cause something as beautiful as the heavens to appear so vile."

"Sir, you speak gravely of the Shadow King and his army, but he has not been seen for many seasons now."

"Not just the Shadow King, young Sir, there are many other evils that lay hidden in those shadows. Some Light, some Dark, some with no allegiance to either."

"Let them answer to this, and we'll see who is hiding in the shadows after that." He held up his Astra Blade, the moonlight reflecting off of it sharply.

The old Knight looked on, smoking his pipe. "Ja, can't argue with that I suppose."

The brash Knight spoke up again, "Come now Karlson, you are being humble in your old age. I have heard all of the stories of you, Shadow Slayer."

"Keep your voice down you fool," Karlson said angrily. "You never know who may be lurking in these shadows."

"If there was a Shadow Knight here I would gut him alive and feed his black heart to my dogs... and wear his tiny shadow of a cock around my neck."

The other Knights laughed at the outspoken Knight's cockiness. All except for Karlson who sat there and shook his head.

"I have seen many Knights finer and stronger than you could ever hope to be young Fredrick, sliced to pieces like they were made of cheese. Those Shadow Blades still keep me awake at night."

Fredrik smiled at Karlson. "Well I know I feel safe with the Shadow Slayer at my back."

The others laughed nervously amongst themselves.

"Well, how about we head back and get ourselves some ale then?" another Knight suggested, finally breaking the tension between them.

"Ja, now that is an idea that I can agree with," Karlson said, as he rose to his feet.

As the Knights began to gather their belongings, Frederik ran over to the forest, only a few yards from where Salazar sat. "Just got to wring out a piss first," he announced, as Karlson watched him with narrowed eyes.

Salazar crept over toward the oblivious pissing Knight and readied his Shadow Blade in his hands. Branches above him shook slightly and caused Frederik to look over. The only noise that followed was the steady stream of urine and once in awhile the soft, muffled whistling of a small bird somewhere in the trees.

Frederik shook off the last drops of his piss, then bent forward to pick up his torch. As his hand reached out for the torch he saw a black blur coming from above. The thud of his arm hitting the ground was the last thing he would hear before the Shadow Blade claimed his head as well.

"Hey, what the hell is going on over there? Frederik?!" Karlson came to check on his fellow knight and stuck his head through the brush. The old Knight stopped in his tracks when he saw Salazar towering over Frederik's lifeless body. Another knight may have screamed, but Karlson was not one of those knights. "You, you do not belong here Shadow Titan. Whoever you are." He spoke calmly and kept his voice low.

Karlson tried to slowly reach to his side where his Astra Blade hung, but Salazar was quick to strike. He rushed toward Karlson, and swung his Shadow Blade down upon the old Knight within a few strides. The Blade mowed through the thick tangle of the forest easily and slashed Karlson's shoulder, through to the bone. Still, the old Knight grabbed Salazar by the cloak and drew him closer, his grip still tenaciously strong as granite despite his mortal wound.

"I will let you die with dignity, Shadow Slayer. Out of respect of who you are, I will make sure that your head remains attached to your body."

"Salazar, it has been many a season since we last locked blades." His voice gurgled, his throat was trying to stop the blood that flooded his mouth.

"On second thought, I owe you nothing, Astra filth." Salazar sneered, as he withdrew his Shadow Blade and swung it over his head. But before he could bring it down on Karlson's neck, the old Knight unsheathed an Ether Glass dagger from his waist and shoved it deep into the ribs of the Titan. Salazar wheeled and screamed, and dropped the Shadow Blade from his hands. The rest of the troop rushed over to see what all the commotion was about and drew their blades when they saw Karlson keeled over as he gurgled his last gasps. Two of them reacted by dropping their blades, and turned to run when they saw Salazar, in all his glory, burst out of the thick brush wielding two enormous Shadow Blades. In one fell swoop, he swung both blades outwards and slashed the throats of the two Knights nearest him. The pair that started to run slowly came back when they saw Salazar slay the others.

"Sir, if you let us leave, I beg of you we have families and—" With one swing Salazar sliced the Knight in twain from head to toe. The remaining Knight screamed and tried to run again but Salazar swung his blade low and cut the Knight's legs off just below his waist.

Salazar collapsed afterward and grasped painfully at his abdomen. Blood spewed from the wound and his cloak was soaked with it. A tree rustled behind him and he looked back again to see what it was. A small bird whistled from within the branches. Salazar turned his attention back to his wound. He wouldn't be able to continue at this rate without treating it. Again the voice came into his head.

"Salazar, your wound, how bad?"

"I need to treat it, or I will bleed out before I even reach the crater."

"Listen to me, that tobakk leaf those men were smoking, if you can find some, cover the wound with it. Then seal them there with a Black Flare spell. It will burn, and hurt immensely but it will hold the wound closed until we can treat it properly."

"I'll try."

Just then a barely there, yet visible glint appeared at the opening of the forest. Salazar squinted to see what the source was, but it was so small that he could not make it out clearly in the darkness of the night. The light grew stronger and stronger as it approached Salazar, and he readied his blades. From behind the light, the small bird whistled once again.

"Stop where you are! Drop those Shadow Blades!" came the voice of a small child. Salazar retracted his blades into his hands and shielded his eyes from the light.

"Are you lost, child? Why don't you put down that light so I can see you?" Salazar asked.

"You do not belong here," the child replied, and with each step that he approached Salazar, the light burned brighter.

"Who is that?" the voice asked.

"Some lost child, I'll dispose of him shortly," Salazar said quietly.

"Get on with it, we need to reach the crater under the cover of darkness."

The child was now within Salazar's reach. He was a young boy, no older than six or seven years, with a small frame and wild red hair as many children of the mountain region had. Salazar then realized that the light was coming from the short Astra dagger that the boy was holding.

"Put that away son, those are very dangerous to play with."

"I saw you kill those Astra Knights, you must pay for that!" the boy screamed and charged at Salazar, taking a wild swing that barely grazed Salazar's cloak. He charged again but Salazar swung his fist and sent the boy flying back and he landed with a thud against the base of a tree. The boy lost consciousness it seemed and the Astra Dagger tumbled out of his hand.

Salazar rose and kicked the blade aside. He held his Shadow Blade high above his head and swung down hard at the boy's body, but before he made contact, he was blown back by the force of his blade being parried, something shielded the boy. When he gathered his senses, he looked over at the man who appeared out of nowhere. He was short in stature, though most were, compared to Salazar. He wore a dark grey tunic that hid his face and hung loosely around his body like a shroud.

"What is happening, Salazar?" the voice inside his head asked.

"I have no fucking idea, but we are not alone here," he spat.

Salazar drew both his Shadow Blades out and circled the man cautiously. He advanced quickly and swung his blade but the man was too agile, and dodged him easily.

"Salazar, who is that?" came the voice again.

Salazar swung his Shadow Blade again and this time it struck, but the man caught the blade in his own orb of black energy and yanked it completely out of Salazar's grasp. The Blade was gone, absorbed by the man's hands. Salazar swung his other blade down but the man countered with a Shadow Staff from between his hands and blocked it. The man leaped up and swung his staff, striking Salazar directly on the head. Salazar staggered backward, stunned. Again the man quickly set upon him and struck over and over at his legs, arms, and body, anywhere that he could not protect. Amidst the onslaught, the hood of the man's tunic fell back and Salazar finally caught a glimpse of his assailant.

"You—" Salazar tried to speak but couldn't.

"What is happening, Salazar?"

"My Liege, he..."

The man lunged again and swung his Shadow Staff hard and low enough to take the feet out from under Salazar, sending him to the ground with a crash so thunderous, the ground shook.

"What is it? Salazar?"

With the wind knocked from him, Salazar wheezed breathlessly, blood pouring from his mouth as he tried to regain his composure. Salazar panted as he tried to speak before the man sent his Shadow Staff directly through the wound that Karlson stabbed earlier. It penetrated through Salazar's body easily and Salazar screamed as he felt his innards being shredded apart, his entrails swung from the end of the staff that pierced through him.

"Scar..." Salazar sputtered before his lifeless body toppled over to the ground.

The Mysterious Warrior

The man stood there with sweat pouring from his brow, a long red scar gashed across his face. He pulled his hood over his head and looked back toward the young boy who still lay beneath the tree. He went over and gathered the Astra Dagger that had fallen from the young boy's grasp. He studied it carefully.

"This is no ordinary blade," he said to himself. He felt the intricate carvings on the handle and marveled at the clarity of the glass. He tucked the dagger away inside of his cloak, taking care not to pierce himself while he did it. He walked over to the young boy, picked him up and slung him over his back. As the boy's head slumped down over his shoulder, a small glass bird that hung around his neck dropped out of his tunic and bounced lightly as they walked. The tail of the bird curled up into what seemed to be some sort of mouthpiece.

"Must be some sort of whistle these people use to communicate," the man said to himself.

"It's a wren," the boy answered, softly. "My father made it for me when I was a babe."

"Why a wren?" the man asked, wondering how long the boy had been awake.

"That's what they call me, in these parts. I've always been smaller than the other boys, so ever since I can remember they've called me Wren."

"Wren," the man repeated, mostly to himself, like he just wanted to get a feel of the word.

"Where are you taking me?" Wren asked after a while.

"I was hoping you could tell me, Wren. Where is your home?"

"I wish not to go there, if that is okay with you, Sir," Wren replied.

"I am no Sir, Wren," the man said darkly. "I am honored that you think so highly of me, but don't confuse me with the distinction of being a Knight."

"My Father was a Knight, it is all I know and I apologize for offending you."

"Was?" the man asked carefully.

"Yes, he was killed, as was my mother. That Shadow Titan came to our village and slaughtered everyone. My father tried to protect us, but the Dark Magick was too much for one man."

"And so you escaped?"

"Yes, I have been tracking the Titan ever since, until you came and slay him."

The man nodded. "Ah, a young Shade Stalker... I too was tracking him. You did very well."

The two continued on silently in the night. Wren fell in and out of sleep while on the man's back. Dawn rolled through the skies in the East. Brilliant pastels of lavender and tangerine blazed through the heavens, as soft, dream-like clouds drifted harmlessly by like ghost ships lost at sea. The man ducked into the trees suddenly and jarred Wren from his slumber. He brought his finger to his lips, before Wren could say a word. Soon Wren heard the hoofs off in the distance also. At least a dozen Shadow Knights rode down the road on black horses and headed in the direction from which they came.

"They are going to retrieve that Titan and extract his blood. It is how they ensure that the Dark Magick stays within the Shadow Kingdom."

Wren nodded. "How do you know all of this?"

"We need to leave now, before more of them start showing up. The Sky Kingdom is no longer safe, Wren," the man said, with no mention of how he came to this knowledge.

The man took one last look in the direction of the Shadow Titan. He bent forward so that Wren could ride again on his back, and they turned and disappeared into the forest.

The Winter Fox

Her figure could be seen for miles, breathtaking and sultry. She arched out of the clean, cool water with an aura of a mythical creature, to catch a glimpse of such beauty would be considered rare and thought-provoking. And yet here she was, for all the world to see. Her long, silver hair flowed down her back akin to the icy tail of a soaring comet, she was like something from another world, from the very heavens itself. Water cascaded down her bare breasts and traced her toned, muscular body which glistened in the morning sun. Colorful fish darted beneath the surface and they grazed her legs as they swam by. A rustle in the bushes signaled where a silver deer emerged and started to graze. It froze as it noticed her standing in the water, but relaxed after a moment, it seemed to trust that she posed it no threat. This was her favorite place to come when she needed some time to herself. Surrounded by the wild foliage of thick, Northern fir trees and enclosed by the base of Mount Himmel, one of the tallest mountains in the White Lions Mountain range. The cool Nordic winds blew through the valley and flowed out into the frozen, eternal tundra.

"Oh, Svela how I do enjoy a good swim first thing in the morning." She turned and covered herself at the sound of the man's voice. She looked around, but there was nothing, only the grazing deer. Svela eyed her longbow back on the shore, well out of her reach, along with her tunic.

"Oh, don't cover up on my behalf, I was enjoying the show."

"Show yourself Jakka!" she yelled into the trees. The deer raised its head and looked around cautiously, sensing the man's presence.

A tall, powerful man jumped down from the branches of one of the trees. He had slick, wavy blonde hair that he brushed back out of his face when he stood up. He wore a dark grey tunic, with a longsword strapped to his back and thin black boots that barely made a sound when he walked. He snickered as Svela tried to keep herself covered in the clear water.

"Can I get you something to dry off with? Or would you like me to take care of that for you?"

She threw her head back and laughed, "Oh wouldn't you like that? Never in your wildest dreams would I ever even consider taking you up on that offer."

"Then you wouldn't want to know what you've already done in my wildest dreams, Svela dear."

"Leave me Jakka, or the Elder will hear about this," she threatened him.

He threw his hands up, feigning his fear. "Now, now. We don't need to get the old man involved, do we?"

"One day that big mouth is going to get you into trouble."

"This?" He pointed at his mouth. "This is average sized compared to the rest of me."

She rolled her eyes. "Leave me Jakka, please, I shall see you back at the League for breakfast."

"If there is one thing I enjoy more than an early morning swim, it is when a beautiful girl begs me for breakfast! Very well, enjoy the rest of your swim and be safe Svela. You never know what dangers lurk in these woods." He laughed again and disappeared back amongst the trees.

Svela exhaled. Jakka was always frustrating to deal with, but especially when she was in such a vulnerable state. He was relentless at times, like a spoiled child. She had known for a while that he fancied her, his gaze was palpable whenever they were together. A woman has a certain intuition when it comes to these things as well, and she was no different. Carnal relations and marriage were strictly prohibited within the League so she had no worry of Jakka ever acting on his feelings, he knew to seek his vices outside of the League. Still, she was definitely put off by him following her, especially when she was alone. She dressed quickly and picked up her longbow. She drew an arrow back and let fly, it screamed through the air and stuck into a low hanging branch, exactly where Jakka had been perched, it should serve as a warning for him next time, she thought. Shooting her bow always helped her relieve any tension. She notched another arrow and turned quickly while firing it straight into a tree on the other side of the lake, narrowly missing a frog's tongue just as it lashed out for its flying prey, her arrow point sticking it first. Svela was far and away the deadliest archer at the League. Her longbow was crafted methodically from the great antlers of the Great Mountain Elk, one of the strongest animals in the White Lions Mountain range. It was light and pliable, allowing her to tirelessly fire multiple arrows over great distances, with pinpoint accuracy.

  The League was all that Svela knew. When she heard tales of other children who could play in the fields from morning to night, she envied them, but for what reason she did not know. She never tried to leave the League, even though they were free to do so if they desired. Where would she even go? She never regretted having to spend her childhood training how to fight, nor did she ever feel disdain toward the League for being what it was. It was her place in the world and she accepted that. Most young girls grew up idolizing their mothers, picking flowers and wearing dresses. Instead, Svela swelled with pride the first time she fired an arrow through a man's heart. She looked back again at the grazing deer, and for a second the great animal stared back at her, it's gentle face gave her a knowing look, one filled with the wisdom of the forests. She gathered her belongings and vaulted from the ground up into the low hanging branch of a nearby fir tree and launched herself, swinging from tree branch to tree branch until eventually she was lost under the great canopy of the forest.

When Svela arrived back at the League, Jakka was already there. He gave her a quick wink as she walked by him at the entrance to the Great Hall. She took her longbow back to her room and changed out of her tunic and into her robes. She examined herself in a mirror that she kept on the wall and brushed her long silver hair free of tangles. Her fair skin clashed beautifully with her deep, black eyes.

There was a whistle at the doorway. "Svela dear, how is it possible that you are even more breathtaking with your clothes on?" Jakka's slippery voice entered the room like a serpent.

"Do you not get tired of harassing me Jakka? You are persistent, I will give you that."

"For beauty like yours, I will persist until my death."

"Now there's an idea. Something I can easily accommodate." She smiled into the mirror.

Before Jakka could reply, footsteps could be heard barreling down the hall toward them. Jakka turned to look, and smiled. A young boy glared at Jakka as he peered into the room.

"My lady Svela, the Elder requests your presence in the Great Hall as soon as you are able to."

"You go run and tell the Elder that Lady Svela is currently busy with Sir Jakka," he said to the boy.

"You are no Sir, Jakka, and Lady Svela has more sense than to associate herself with the likes of you." To this Svela turned and laughed.

"Young Wren is wiser than his years show, you should listen to him Jakka, it will save you much strife."

Jakka sneered at Wren. "Listen, boy, you should keep your little beak out of other people's business," he said, his tone harsh. "Go now, run along and play."

Wren cowered away from Jakka. "I-I, I am to escort Lady Svela to the Great Hall, where the Elder awaits her company," he managed to say without looking up.

"Well, I think I'll just have to take you up on that offer, Wren. You never know what dangers lurk in these halls," she said, looking sideways at Jakka.

Wren stepped in toward Svela to take her arm, but Jakka reached in front and shoved Wren hard against the stone wall. The young boy fell to his knees, winded at the sudden jarring. Svela glared at Jakka and knelt down to make sure Wren was alright.

"Oh he'll be fine, he's a big boy. Aren't you Wren?"

Jakka went to help Wren up but the young boy tore his arm away from him, determined to stand under his own strength. As he was getting back to his feet, Jakka stuck his giant boot out, kicking Wren back down to the ground.

"Asshole," Svela said, shaking her head. Jakka threw his hands up in the air, smirking.

This time Wren lunged at Jakka, throwing his fists in every direction. Jakka sidestepped him with ease and grabbed the young boy by his throat and pinned up against the wall. Wren flailed, trying to escape from Jakka's grip, but Jakka was much too strong.

"If you ever try that again, I will slice you in half, I promise you this, little bird."

"Jakka, put the boy down."

Jakka turned to find Ragnvar looming in the doorway.

The man surprised Svela with his stealth, even now as he was standing still his movements were smooth and calculated. He wore long black robes, not unlike the ones that Svela and Jakka were wearing. His eyes were serious and cold and even

Jakka smiled but did not say a word. He dropped Wren down to the floor with a thud.

"Ragnvar! So nice of you to join us, Brother! I was just giving young Wren over here some field training." He held out his hand to Ragnvar, who looked down at it and then back up at Jakka without any sort of acknowledgment.

"Come on, he is a little shit squire, and he is always underfoot."

"He is a member of the League, Jakka. We all started here as squires when we were younger, don't ever forget that. We all have our place." Jakka watched as Ragnvar turned and started to walk away and spat on the ground in front of Wren, before he turned and left himself.

Wren stood up and yelled down the hall, "Thank you Ragnvar!"

"Stay out of Jakka's way, Wren. I won't always be there to help you," Ragnvar said without turning around.

"My lady, the Elder still awaits us." But Svela was still staring back down the hall at Ragnvar as he walked away.

"My lady?" Wren said again.

"Yes, my apologies Wren. We should not keep the Elder."

She took one last look down the hall, but Ragnvar had already disappeared. Wren watched Svela as she did this and smiled.

"I saw my Lady's eyes light up when Sir Ragnvar came by."

Svela looked down at Wren. "No, it's not like that Wren. I, don't know how to explain it to you, it's beyond your years."

"Jakka is quite fond of you; he has the same look in his eyes when my Lady is present."

Svela laughed. "Now I know for sure that you don't understand, Wren."

When they both arrived at the Great Hall the Elder was already sitting at the end of the long dining table that stretched across the entire room. He was slight in stature now, and his grey tunic hung off of him loosely. Svela had noticed lately how aged he had become, right before her eyes. He still welcomed them with the same warm eyes, and the same compassionate smile she had known for years.

"Svela, dear, so nice to see you. Wren, thank you for going to get her for me."

"Of course My Lord. I am yours to command, now and always." Wren bowed his head to the Elder.

"Would you do me another favor Wren, and go fetch Ragnvar and Jakka. I need to speak to the three of them in private."

Wren bowed again deeply, and ran off with a quiet patter.

The Elder turned to Svela, "He is a good squire, and a quick learner. I am just not sure if he will ever have the stature that is needed."

"My Lord, might I remind you many a time you told me stories of how you grew from the same place, and yet you overcame that to be one of the most feared warriors in all the realm."

"Please, Svela, no need for such formalities when the others are not present. I am no Lord, I have told you this before."

"Forgive me, Father, but I wish not to have any special treatment because I am your daughter."

The Elder smiled and chuckled softly. "You are a true soldier, Svela, I would never dream of giving you any preference in the eyes of others. You are the strongest woman I have ever known, and I take pride in how I raised you, so forgive me for thinking of you as unique, but you always will be special to your dear old father. You must never forget that Old, Noble blood runs through your veins, your prowess with the longbow and your bravery in battle are proof of that."

To this, she couldn't help but smile. "Everything that I am I owe to you Father, I hope you know this. What is so urgent that you felt the need to call Ragnvar and Jakka?" Remembering what her Father had asked of Wren.

"I have just received word from a member of the Shadow King's Counsel. They need us to dispose of a troop of Lunar Knights that seized shipments from across the Narvik Sea." He stopped when he saw the disappointed look on Svela's face.

"Why do we continue to help the Shadow King? We are just furthering his reach into the realm. More people will die, every time that we help him."

"Svela, dear. We are impartial, we take no side, but we have our place."

"Yes, I know Father, I am reminded every day of my life of this."

"Then why do you not understand that this is a job, separate of any political allegiances. The Astra King leaves just as many corpses in his wake."

"Yes, but we know the Shadow Kingdom and what they represent. The Shadow Knights are truly evil, I have seen them commit atrocities that I could never even imagine, except for that I have witnessed with my own eyes. And who orders them what to do?"

"That is not of our concern, Svela."

"It is the concern of the realm, Father."

"That is enough," the Elder said sternly.

"Oh my, now I know where Svela gets her temper from," Jakka said as he entered the room with Wren and Ragnvar.

"My Lord," Ragnvar said, bowing deeply on one knee.

Jakka looked over at him and rolled his eyes, saying, "Oh right, sorry My Lord" and he bent down to one knee alongside Ragnvar.

Svela stormed out of the Dining Hall, she could be heard cursing and screaming down the halls as she left.

The Elder

"That is some fury you raised her with, My Lord," Jakka said, when Svela could no longer be heard.

The Elder nodded and said, "She will have to learn to keep her emotions under control. One day it may be the difference between life and death, not just for her but for all of us."

"Let me speak to her, my Lord, perhaps she needs to hear it as a suggestion from a peer rather than as an order from her Father," Jakka volunteered.

"Thank you Jakka, I will take your suggestion under advisement for now. If the three of you will accompany me back to my chambers, I have received a mission for you to carry out."

"Three of us?" repeated Jakka. "Since when do squires get to sit in on mission briefings?" He looked down at Wren.

"Since I have invited him, Jakka. Wren has proven that he earned the right to play a bigger role in the League."

"Let us stop quibbling about such trivial matters, it makes no difference to me if the boy is present or not," Ragnvar said.

"Stay out of my way, boy. Or I will not be accountable for the flesh that my blade finds in the heat of battle." Jakka sneered.

Wren watched as the Elder slowly unraveled a parchment and the remnants of the black wax seal of the Shadow Kingdom flaked off and fell to the ground. The three of them listened intently as the Elder began to read the contents of the letter.

> *To whom it may concern,*
> *I write this letter to you as a member of the King's Council on behalf of the great Shadow King, ruler of the Shadow Kingdom and rightful King of the realm. I am requesting your assistance in the disposal of a troop of Knights from the Lunar Kingdom of Mane. They are situated in the Port City of Narvik about a day's march outside of Mane and have seized a shipment of slaves and other materials from across the Narvik Sea. Leave none alive and claim what rightfully belongs to the Shadow Kingdom. A troop of Shadow Knights will meet you just outside of the town proper for further instruction.*

"Narvik? Curious. When do we leave?" Ragnvar asked.

"The whores in those Lunar Kingdom towns are excellent, I do remember that," Jakka added.

"Yes, well. I have already informed Svela of the mission."

"And what about him?" Jakka nodded toward Wren, interrupting the Elder.

"Ultimately, I will leave it up to the three of you if young Wren is to accompany you. In my eyes, he is more than capable."

"I am more concerned with why a troop of Shadow Knights needs our help with this simple job," Ragnvar said.

The Elder looked over at Ragnvar. "I think it is a test. A test of our allegiance and our abilities. The Shadow King makes no move without strategizing beforehand."

"Well, whatever the reason may be, you can count me in. My blade is thirsty these days," Jakka added.

Ragnvar nodded. "Make your preparations tonight, we shall leave at dawn." And with that, he turned to leave.

"What about the boy?" Jakka called after him.

"Let him come, if he doesn't get in our way." Wren's eyes lit up when he heard this.

"I will not be responsible for him," Jakka said to the Elder, before making his exit.

"If I may have a word with you Young Wren, before you leave to prepare."

"Yes, of course, my Lord."

"Ten years now. It's been ten years since I found you in that forest. Do you remember much from that night?"

Wren nodded. "I remember it all, My Lord. I shall never forget it."

"Good. My daughter, in all her wisdom, reminded me that I was once very much like you, Wren. I was never the largest boy, and I was never the strongest. But what I lacked in brawn I made up for in intelligence and ability. I trained every day, from dawn until dusk. I worry about you, Wren. I think of you now as my own child, and I question myself every day whether or not it is time for you to graduate from being a squire. It would mean not just that you would be sent on missions, with Ragnvar and Jakka and Svela, but that you would be free to leave the League if you wished to find your place."

"I have nowhere to go, My Lord, I couldn't dream of leaving, my place is here," Wren pleaded.

The Elder nodded. "You say this now, young Wren. Soon, as you begin to explore the realm on your own you may realize that this life is not for you. I want you to listen to me. Stay with Sir Ragnvar. I fear for the life of anyone that follows Jakka into battle. Be wary around him, there is a darkness inside of that young man that we still have not seen," the Elder said gravely.

"I also fear I have not equipped you as well as I could have. You lack the archery skills of Svela or the proficiency with blades that Jakka and Ragnvar possess. I am telling you, Wren, to keep the Astra Blade that your Father made you close at hand."

Wren nodded and placed his hand instinctively on the handle of the dagger that he carried on his belt. "I will, My Lord."

"You are a smart boy Wren, and I have a feeling that your role in this world will be larger than you think." The Elder paced the floor with his hands clasped behind his back.

"My Lord, I fear Sir Ragnvar is not quite fond of me. How do I win his praises?"

"Young boy, Sir Ragnvar is not fond of anybody. I warned you about Jakka, I should give you fair warning of Sir Ragnvar as well. His is a darkness I have witnessed. Stand by his side but stay clear of his sword, or he will not hesitate to amputate you from himself. There is no head Sir Ragnvar will not take if it stands in his way, and he will do so without remorse."

Wren remained silent, taking in all that the Elder was telling him.

"I have faith in you son, do not make me regret it. I sense a light inside of you that will lead us when we are blinded. Now, time to prepare yourself for your first mission. Get yourself a good night of rest, Sir Ragnvar waits for no one."

***

In the morning, Wren equipped himself with what he could. He knelt down to one knee and held the small glass bird that he wore around his neck, kissing it.

"Protect me Mother, Father. Keep me in your light and protect me from any darkness that I may encounter, friend or foe."

He tucked it back under his tunic, grabbed his dagger and sword and headed out to meet the rest of the party.

Sir Ragnvar and Jakka were already mounted on their horses by the time Wren came outside. Ragnvar on a brilliant black stallion, that made him appear even more imposing than usual. Jakka and Svela rode equally impressive steeds that stood calmly as they waited for Wren.

"Hurry up boy; we are already late because of you," Jakka yelled from atop his horse.

Wren ran over to the small white mule that another squire was bringing out from the stables. Wren looked at the animal and then looked back at the Elder.

"Is this for me?" he asked.

The Elder nodded. "He is obedient and surefooted, never underestimate the importance of a good mule."

But Wren could already hear Jakka snickering at him.

"Is he going to be able to keep up with us?" Jakka asked Svela.

"Shut up Jakka, leave him alone."

The mule brayed loudly as Wren approached it and flicked its ears once or twice at him.

"Easy now." Wren reached out and stroked the mule softly on its muzzle. "There, that's not so bad now is it?" The mule calmed instantly, and even nuzzled its face next to Wren's after a while.

"Look at that Wren, you are a natural!" said Svela with a smile.

"Let us go," Ragnvar said. "I do not like the looks of the sky in the East." He nodded toward the horizon, where the sun had risen. The clouds were full and the sky was brazen with red and orange. "Blood has been drawn this night."

"Godspeed to all of you," the Elder spoke up. He walked over to each of them and spoke. Wren listened intently as he waited for the Elder to approach him.

"Jakka, lead your blade with your courage, be mindful of your mouth being guided by your heart. I know of very few in this realm that can match your skills with a sword, and I know of none who can match your arrogance or wit. Keep your brothers and sisters safe, and return to me as the warrior I know you are. I bestow upon you the name of the Jackal, heard before they are seen, vicious and relentless."

Jakka bowed his head. "I will, my Lord." Next, the Elder walked over to Svela.

"Svela, protect your brothers with your longbow and your heart. Be the peacemaker, keep Jakka under control and always have an eye out for Young Wren. Return to me, my daughter, as the warrior that I know you are. I bestow upon you, my dear, the name of the Winter Fox, quick and cunning. Listen, and strike before being seen."

Svela bowed her head, and said the same, "I will, my Lord."

"Young Wren, my son. I pray for you the most. Remember what I told you, stay next to Sir Ragnvar. Keep one eye on what is behind you at all times and protect yourself from Jakka's words, or more. You will be the light that will guide us home. Return to me as the warrior that I know you are. I bestow upon you the name of Wren, the name you were birthed with, honest and true, keen of sight, sharp of mind."

Wren felt his eyes fill with tears; he bowed his head and mumbled, "I will, My Lord."

Finally, the Elder walked over to Sir Ragnvar.

"Sir Ragnvar, I entrust in you the lives of my sons and daughter. Protect your brothers and your sister and protect this realm from the darkness that will soon come. Watch for young Wren, he is green and raw but he has a usefulness that will one day serve its purpose. Keep both ears and eyes out for Jakka, his combination of skill and attitude make him very dangerous for foe and friend alike. Return to me as their leader, and as the warrior that I know you are. I bestow upon you the name of Viper, the silent death; a Viper will do what must be done."

Wren watched as Jakka eyed the Elder as he spoke to Ragnvar longer than the others. For a brief moment, as the Elder leaned into Ragnvar, he looked back and his eyes locked with Jakka's. Jakka smiled but then turned away.

***

The four of them rode in silence through the endless flatlands of the Lundmark Tundra that stretched across most of the continent. It was mostly a straight route to Narvik, two days by horseback would get them there in plenty of time. Faster and faster the mighty stallions pushed their thunderous hooves through the cold, icy earth. When they stopped to rest their horses, they kept to the side of the mighty Junta River that flowed through the length of the tundra from the Narvik Sea to the icecaps on the very tops of the White Lions Mountains, the crests of the ranges resembling that of a lion mane. The horses drank thirstily from the cool, crisp water as the four stood around and fed them a bag of wild green apples that Wren foraged from the nearby woods.

Svela sat nearby with her feet in the river, whittling some arrows out of discarded deer antlers that had been strewn around the ground.

Ragnvar and Jakka sat together discussing where to break for camp for the night. They sat sharpening their blades with coarse rocks found on the beds of the river. Wren listened in as he fed and watered the horses.

"What say you Jakka? Over the hills to the East lies the Lunar Kingdom and I would prefer not to camp there overnight. Ideally, we would ride right through, so as not to bring any attention to ourselves."

"I say we can handle a troop of Lunar Knights, brother, even with the boy. It may be best to get as far as we can today then camp in the cover of the forest."

"Fair enough Jakka, you know I always hold your strategic eye in high esteem. This time I do believe we will be better off entering quietly. We may have already been spotted for all we know."

"And I say stop being so timid, brother. They are no match for us, you know this."

"Never underestimate your enemy Jakka, it is a sure way to meet defeat."

"It hasn't happened yet. Do not underestimate your own brother either. I have confidence in my blade."

"I have confidence in your blade as well Jakka, perhaps even more than in my own. But I will not risk the safety of Svela or Wren just so we can claim glory to our blades. As leader of this mission, I forbid it. We will head for the cover of the forest for tonight, and make our way into Lunar land come morning."

"Fine, if that is your command, brother, I will obey it." Jakka went on sharpening his blade, but Ragnvar watched him. "A few more hours of riding and we should be able to reach the wooded area over the hills. The horses seem to be done feeding, for now, gather yourselves and let us ride." He rose and walked over to untie his steed.

Wren brought over Svela's horse but she did not notice as she scanned the horizon intently. She leaned forward and narrowed her eyes, while cocking her head slightly to listen.

"Let us approach quietly, Sir Ragnvar, there is a movement beyond those trees. The birds are always honest about danger nearby."

Ragnvar nodded. "Well scouted Svela, let us cross the river here and enter the forest from the rear. I do not want to risk any sort of ambush."

"Let them come to me," Jakka said, swinging his blade silently through the air. "Just let them try and trap us."

Ragnvar glared at Jakka, but Jakka went on silently slaying the imaginary foes.

"We cannot ride across, it is too deep. Guide your horse across there, where it is most shallow. "

Svela led first, her silver horse reared when its hooves dipped into the ice-cold water. She stroked its neck gently and pulled its head along surely with the reins. In a few seconds, she was across, and Jakka followed closely behind her.

"Go ahead Wren," Ragnvar said to him as the other two crossed.

Wren took one step in and then another. The water chilled him to the bone; his feet were numb and ached from the cold. His mule felt it too, and though Wren tried to stroke its neck just as he had seen Svela do, the mule began to panic as the water reached its knees.

"Wren, control him. Pull by the reins, guide its head," Ragnvar called out from behind, but it was too late.

The mule brayed, kicking wildly, and just like that, Wren was no longer in control. He tried to maintain his footing on the slippery rocks but the reins ripped from his grasp just as he lost balance and fell deep into the raging current. Screams came from above the surface but he had lost his senses in the ice cold water, he was gasping for air within seconds. The water swept him furiously along at great speeds and twice he knocked his head against jagged rocks, bloodying the water. He sank under, being pulled along for what seemed like an eternity, and tossed around at the river's mercy like he was a child's toy. The Elder was right to be worried about him. Maybe he wasn't cut out for this; perhaps he should have just stayed back at the League as a squire, sharpening swords and feeding the horses. He felt humiliated now; they would probably just let him die now so as not to slow them down for the rest of the mission.

Just then, a strong, hard grip grasped him under the arm and instantly his lungs filled with air again as he was thrown onto the shore. He gasped and coughed up water and vomited all over himself, but he was slightly pleased that he hadn't shit himself during the frenzy.

"Wren, are you alright?"

But Wren could not answer yet, his mouth was still filled with vomit and blood, and his head was disoriented. Someone was shaking him, but his eyes were still unfocused.

"Wren! Wake up, boy!"

When he finally came to, he saw Jakka staring down at him, with a smile on his face.

"There we go! I knew you were tougher than that. He's okay!" he called over to Svela and Ragnvar, who were tending to Wren's mule.

"You saved me?" Wren managed to ask.

"You can buy me a whore in Narvik if it makes you feel better," Jakka replied.

Ragnvar had walked over. "Wren, you'll ride with Jakka, I will tie your mule to my horse and guide it. We have lost some time now and we need to make it to those woods by sunset."

"Are you alright Wren?" Svela asked with a concerned look on her face. She and Jakka helped Wren up and lifted him onto Jakka's horse.

"Let us ride; we have already wasted enough time here," Ragnvar said, as he rode off.

"Nice to see how concerned our fearless leader is," Jakka said to Svela as they mounted their horses.

"He has to think about all of us and the mission, Jakka, it is a great burden to undertake."

"Yes, and maybe if you stopped thinking about his cock, you would see what an ass he is." Jakka turned and rode off. Wren looked back and heard Svela sigh to herself as she shook her head, then set off behind them for the forest.

If you're enjoying this story, please leave a review for League of Assassins by clicking here.

The Viper

Darkness fell by the time they reached the woods.

Ragnvar chose to set up a camp in a nice clearing that was reinforced from the back by a rocky cliffside. He watched as Jakka and Svela approached the clearing and tied up their horses.

"Where is Wren?" Svela asked.

"I have sent him out to gather firewood and forage for some food," Ragnvar replied without looking up at her.

"You could have let him rest, Ragnvar."

"He said he was fine," Ragnvar said, dismissing Svela.

"Of course he is going to say that, but he almost drowned back at the river."

Ragnvar stopped and looked over at Svela. He saw that she averted her eyes when he laid his upon her. "But he didn't," he said firmly, as if to end the matter.

Svela groaned in frustration and glared back at Ragnvar. "I am going out to help him then." She turned off towards the woods, before Ragnvar had a chance to reply.

Jakka chuckled from where he sat, pulling off his boots. "Brother, you do have a way with the women."

Ragnvar ignored his comment. "Jakka, you stay here in case they come back, I am going to go, scout, the area, and see if there are any signs of movement that Svela spotted earlier."

Jakka was lying down on his back now. "Sure, go have fun Ragnvar. I may be deep into my slumber by the time you return. Be sure not to wake me if I am moaning."

"Keep an eye on the horses Jakka, and an ear out for Wren and Svela."

"Sure, I'll do just that," Jakka said, but his eyes were already closed.

Ragnvar made his way quickly through the forest, as he used the giant Northern Fir trees as cover. He paused for a brief second; he placed his ear to the ground and listened intently at the direction of the footsteps that he tracked. The Elder would be disappointed in him, Ragnvar thought. They almost lost Wren in the river and now he sent Wren and Svela off into the woods on their own. He picked up his pace and drew his blades when he heard the voices of men off in the distance.

The Wren

Wren stumbled through the dark as he gathered firewood to bring back for the camp. He stubbed his toe on wild roots that reached up at him out of the earth, and almost tripped twice. His head still ached from the river and he shivered right down to his bones as his damp clothes weren't dried at all. Each step he took, water squished out of his boots and his feet started to itch inside of the dampened lining.

Suddenly he stopped dead in his tracks. Up ahead, six torches floated ominously in the darkness, and as they came closer the sound of men's voices filled the night air.

"They should be here soon, keep an eye out. Three large horses and a shit mule aren't easy to hide in these woods," a man's voice rasped.

Another man spoke, "You all can do what you wish with the men, that silver-haired whore is mine and I want her alive."

"Oi, I want a turn at her too, never fucked me a woman that has killed before."

Wren crouched down behind some bushes and lay the firewood down quietly. He listened as the footsteps came near.

"This is my chance to redeem myself," he whispered to himself. He grabbed the handle of his dagger and drew it from his belt. The clear glass blade pierced the darkness with its radiance.

"What was that?" one of the men said suddenly, the footsteps had stopped.

Wren sank down lower, but the blade was so bright that it glowed even through his tunic.

"I saw something flashing over there in those bushes."

"Oi, I saw it too, someone's there!"

One of the men drew his sword, and then slowly walked over to the bushes. He stabbed his blade wildly, hitting nothing except leaf and branch, with a shrug, he then peered around the bushes, but when he looked there was nothing there.

"There's just a bunch of wood back here, looks like someone was gathering it earlier." He walked back behind the pile of wood and kicked a few pieces into the bushes.

"Ain't nothing else back he—" But before he could finish his words, his throat gurgled with blood as Wren drove the blade up through his neck and into the man's mouth. He dropped like a sack of stones, lifeless.

"Oi, quit fuckering around! Are ya fingerin' yourself back there?" another man called out, but there was no response. "Something is off, bring over some light!" The other men charged into the clearing with fire and Wren quickly darted around the trees to escape, but his dagger gleamed fiercely in the firelight. One of the men spotted him easily and yelled out.

"There, a child or something around that tree!"

The other men pursued Wren through the darkness, he had sheathed his dagger, blotting out its brilliance. Their torches came closer and closer to him, but he couldn't move quickly enough, his feet were blistered from the wet boots he had been trudging around in. As if by the mere thought of cursing his boot, he felt it hit something hard on the ground and suddenly, he tumbled head over feet into the bramble with a loud crash.

"The little shit fell, I've got him!"

He felt the man grab his arms with his hands and roughly yank him, bringing him back up to his feet.

"He's just a boy!" The man lifted him and carried him over to the others.

"Who are you, boy? Who are you here with?" asked one of the men.

Wren spat at them and refused to say a word.

"You little shit." The man punched him clear in the jaw, then raised his blade to Wren's throat. "I should gut you now and—"

There was the sound of a whistling in the air... then the man dropped to his knees and gushed blood skyward, as did the man behind him. Two fountains of blood sprayed, as the others watched on. Another hard bone arrow screamed through the night and skewered two, both through the head in one shot. The other man dropped Wren and chaos broke out as the three remaining men tried to run. One crashed to the ground in moments, as an arrow entered through one side of his neck, and out the other. The other two managed to escape into the forest but the unmistakable sound of two blades being drawn and slicing through human flesh announced their fates.

Svela jumped down from a tree behind Wren, and seconds later a shadow emerged from out of the woods. It was Ragnvar, wiping clean his blood-drenched blades.

"Wren, are you alright?" Svela asked.

"Yes, I'm fine." But he trembled uncontrollably, his hands shook violently under his tunic and he could still smell the blood of the man he slew earlier.

"You must be wary of where you venture, Wren. From what I could see they were the only troop in the area," Ragnvar said. "Let us head back to camp and get some rest. Wren, pick up the firewood."

***

Ragnvar took first watch that night as he usually did. Sleep was something that would take time away from his practice and meditation, he believed it to be for the weak. He sat still in the darkness and quietly smoked a tobakk pipe as the others slept. It was clear and silent, not even the animals stirred on this night. He was thankful that Wren and Svela were safe, but that was two close calls in one day, this is why he preferred doing assignments alone, but perhaps he was being too harsh on Wren. This mission was too dangerous for his leadership to falter.

He heard a small rustle behind him.

"I cannot sleep," Wren's voice piped up as he made his way over to where Ragnvar sat.

"Of all of us you need the most rest, Wren. You have had a long day."

"I-I can't. My hands keep shaking."

"Are you still cold from the river? I told you to dry your boots and tunic by the fire."

"No," Wren shook his head. "It's not that. I killed that man, and all I see when I close my eyes is the look on his face, as his life slowly slipped away." His voice trembled as he said this. "I keep wondering... if he had a son or a daughter..."

Ragnvar remained silent for a moment, he inhaled deeply into his pipe, and the embers glowed faintly in the darkness.

"It is something you will have to get used to, Wren," Ragnvar finally said, looking down into his pipe, then not knowing what else to do, he offered it to Wren.

"How can I? Perhaps I was not cut out for this, Jakka was right." Wren looked at the pipe with wide eyes, but shook his head.

"Perhaps he was, Wren. Time will tell. The Elder believes in you and for me, that is enough."

This time it was Wren who remained silent, reaching out for the pipe, and in one motion, taking a small quick puff; he looked to Ragnvar for approval.

Ragnvar took back the pipe, and could not help but smile; perhaps one of the first Wren had seen, directed at him.

But the moment was brief, Wren coughed hard, expelling the puff of smoke from his virgin lungs. He spent a good minute, hacking up what he thought were his very intestines, but nothing came out. Ragnvar slapped him hard on the back, helping him to clear his breath.

Finally, when his breathing was calm, he spoke, "Jakka saved me today from the river. Why? I thought he would be happy to let me drown and be done with me."

"Jakka is complicated to understand. His mouth betrays him usually, but somewhere under there he has a good heart. He jumped into the river of his own volition, nobody told him to do that."

"I don't want to be a burden to you or anyone anymore, Sir Ragnvar."

"Then don't be. Prove to me that you belong with us. Killing that man tonight was a good first step, now clear your conscience because I promise you, Wren, there will be many more lives taken by your hand before the end of it."

"I will try," Wren said shakily.

"The Elder told me in confidence that he knows you will serve a purpose one day. What that purpose is, we do not know. But I intend to keep you alive until we find out what it is."

Wren smiled widely. "That sounds fine to me, Sir Ragnvar. Tell me about your first kill, did it bother you like it does me?"

"It does, to this very day, Wren. The feel of my blade cutting through living flesh, that sensation never leaves you. The smell of blood and death permeates through your soul, your skin, your very fiber. It is never easy, Wren. It never becomes easy. This feeling will pass, and one day you will learn how to deal with it. One day you will realize that this is the road that you have been given."

Wren nodded silently. "Before, when I couldn't sleep, all I could see were my parents being murdered in cold blood by the Shadow Titan Salazar. That was just before the Elder found me alone in the woods. I had been wandering for days, I was hungry and I was weak. When I came to, the Elder had defeated Salazar, and offered to take me home." Wren paused. "But I didn't know where home was anymore."

Wren paused, waiting for Ragnvar to respond but he didn't. "Do you remember how you came to the League, Sir Ragnvar?"

"No, I don't remember. I was too young." Silently he drew a long toke off of his pipe.

The two sat together, and not another word was shared. The sun began to rise in front of them and brilliant hues of orange and pink sprayed across the sky. Jakka and Svela rose from their slumber as Ragnvar and Wren fed and watered the horses and prepared them for the day's voyage.

"I am starved like a babe waitin' for a mother's tit," Jakka announced as he rummaged through his tunic for any foods. "Ideally a very well-endowed mother," he mumbled to himself.

"There are some apples that you can wrestle the horses for," Svela said with a smirk.

"Svela dear, what say you to an early morning swim together?"

"Why Jakka, I'd rather drown myself in the river."

"We will forage for food on our way out of the forest," Ragnvar said. "I saw some quail nests last night and a patch of wild mushrooms we could eat."

"Oh my, you spoil us Sir Ragnvar." Jakka rolled his eyes.

"Find your own food, Jakka, I am not your servant."

The City of Narvik

The City of Narvik was gated heavily. From its natural entry point as a port town on a sharp peninsula that jutted out into the Narvik Sea, it acted as the portal to the main continent. Security was high here, and armed Lunar Knights patrolled the outer reaches of the city. Narvik Castle could be seen high above the walls, and the high architecture and rose-gold walls flaunted the port city's wealth. The four of them watched from the edge of the forest and learned the timing of the guard's routes.

"Strange, we are supposed to liaise with a troop of Shadow Knights before we enter the City," Ragnvar remarked.

Wren turned to look and caught Svela and Ragnvar sharing a look.

Jakka spoke, without looking away from the gates, "They will be here, I am sure of it."

"Halt, who is that up there? Show your faces!" a man's voice barked from behind, when they turned to look there was an entire troop of Lunar Knights closing in on them.

"Shit, an ambush! We've been set up!" Jakka screamed as he drew his curved longsword.

In a hushed whisper, Ragnvar barked, "Split up, meet back at the camp!" He unsheathed his dual blades, preparing for battle.

Wren ran back toward the men to distract them. He readied his dagger, the glass reflected the glare of the sun, blinding the men temporarily. Out of the corner of his eye, Wren saw the end of Svela's silver hair disappear into the trees. He looked back and saw Jakka as he swung his longsword and laughed like a madman. He struck down Knights left and right, blood splattering across his face like a ravenous animal. Moving from one to another so quickly, and ferociously.

"Come and get it you savages, there is plenty of my blade to go around." A large Knight charged him and knocked Jakka backwards into a tree. The Knight raised his Warhammer ax and swung it down at him, but Jakka was too quick. He rolled back into the legs of the Knight and the Warhammer smashed through the tree trunk as if it were made of glass, splintered wood flew in every direction. Jakka stabbed upward with all of his might, jamming his blade underneath the man's helmet, directly into this throat. The Knight staggered backwards and toppled over, dead.

"Jakka! Run, there are too many of them!" Ragnvar's voice was strained as he fought off Knight after Knight. He skewered two in the gut, one with each blade, then just pulled them out in time to slash the throats of two other Knights that rushed at him.

Wren kept running, he wanted to get back to his mule and ride back to the League, he felt terrified and he was sick of being weak. Two Knights chased him through the brush and he ducked in and out of the trees but could not lose them. As he ran he heard two arrows whiz by his head, when he looked back he saw both of the Knights impaled against trees. Wren smiled. Svela never missed her shots. Through the forest, he still could hear Ragnvar and Jakka as they sliced through flesh as if it were a butcher's shop. Svela jumped down from a tree up ahead and joined Wren.

"Where are we? What direction is our camp?" Svela called out to Wren.

"This way! I can hear the river this way!" Wren replied, out of breath from running.

Wren stopped. He watched as Svela veered off to follow him she was blindsided by two more Knights, crashing into her. She hit the ground hard, and lay there groaning.

"Look at this pretty little thing, with the nice silver hair," the Knight to the left said.

"Take a look at the longbow she is carrying."

Wren stalked the two men as they closed in on Svela. As the first Knight went to pick up Svela's longbow, Wren took his chance. Pouncing forward, he rolled across the ground and slashed at the backs of the legs of the Knight closest to him, and the large man howled in pain as he fell to the ground. The other

Knight whipped around and spotted Wren running past him. He turned to give chase, but ran right into Ragnvar's blade, where it sliced his torso in half. Ragnvar ran over to Svela and threw her over his shoulder.

"Wren, I lost track of Jakka, go and find him. Meet us back at the camp."

"Yes, Sir Ragnvar!"

Wren dashed back to where he last saw Jakka. All was silent now, he had to carefully step over corpses wherever he walked. The bottoms of his boots were sticky from the blood and vitriol that covered the ground and the smell of death permeated through the air. Carrion birds were starting to circle overhead; this bloodbath left a feast for scavengers, carrion feeders and others of their ilk. Wren doubled back to the perimeter of the forest where the group was first spotted by the Knights. He walked quietly and made sure to stay within the trees so as not to be caught again. Wren traced his steps from battle and came upon the tree that the large Knight had smashed with the Warhammer. He examined the trunk and shuddered at the destructive power of such a weapon. A few yards from the tree he found the large Knight lying in a pool of his own blood, the Warhammer just out of reach of his cold grasp. As he circled behind the smashed tree, he followed the path of destruction. More Knights slaughtered like pigs, Jakka was truly efficient with his blade and Wren marveled at the warrior he could be.

"I wonder if Sir Ragnvar could even defeat Jakka in a duel," he whispered to himself, as he passed over some more victims.

Wren stopped suddenly when he heard muted voices coming from within the forest. His hand instinctively grasped the handle of his dagger, and he dropped down to the ground so as not to be seen. He quietly crawled along until he was able to hide himself within a row of bushes. From within the bushes, Wren spotted several figures standing in a small clearing. He couldn't quite make out the faces but he could count at least eight men wearing black hooded cloaks and armed with long swords with thick blades that were cold and black as death. One of them spoke with his voice raised, but the voice who answered that froze Wren in his place.

It was Jakka.

"You cannot blame me for your troop's incompetence. I do not know how much more help you need." Jakka was his usual pompous self.

The leader of the troop spoke up, "Leave it up to the Lunar Knights to fumble everything. Too much gold, and not enough brains for that lot." His voice was low and raspy, like his throat was full of rusted knives.

"Well, either way, I believe I am owed some gold. There was no specification of whether or not you fools succeeded or failed."

The leader handed Jakka a small sack. "Feels a bit light, are you sure it's all in there?" Jakka lightly tossed the sack in his hand up and down.

"It's all there Jakka, you need not worry about that."

"Pleasure doing business with you lads, don't get any ideas trying to take this gold from me now."

"Send word when you arrive back at the League. We will need you for another contract shortly. This time, the stakes will be higher. The King is ready to mobilize and there is a plan in place. This is going to be big, Jakka, more than any sack of gold can get you."

Jakka turned and looked back in the direction of Wren. Wren's heart hammered in his chest, and he put his head down onto the ground so as not to make a sound. Jakka turned back toward the Shadow Knights after a moment.

"The four of us will be riding back to the League on the same path, alongside the banks of the Junta River. Let us ride freely, I see no reason for you to interject there."

"We shall be watching from afar. The child, what does he mean to the League? We have never seen him on a mission before."

Wren listened intently, they were being watched? He wondered to himself.

"He is just a boy, just like you said. The Elder is high on him, and the Viper seems to be warming to him. Why?" Jakka asked.

"No reason, yet. If the Elder and the Viper treasure him so, he may make a fine bargaining chip in the future."

Jakka laughed. "He is slippery and he has a fire in his belly. I am not so sure you should take him lightly. He has been trained at the League since he was a child, meaning soon he'll be able to handle himself with the likes of any of you lot."

The Shadow Knights bristled, and several of them drew their black blades, and pointed them at Jakka.

Jakka laughed. "Do not embarrass yourselves, your heads will hit the ground before you lay a scratch on me."

The Shadow Knights maintained their stances while their leader stepped back, out of the fray.

Jakka shrugged his shoulders. "If you insist."

Four of the Shadow Knights charged with their blades but before they could even reach Jakka, he jumped straight into the air and spun forcefully with his longsword, taking with him four black hooded heads. The lifeless bodies collapsed to the ground in unison. The leader raised his hand when the other three Shadow Knights drew their blades.

"Enough, you fools, you are no match. Put your weapons away. You have proven your point Jakka, now leave us. This plan was foiled, but the next one will not be. Send word when you can."

Jakka waved his blade. "Last chance boys, I am always up for a fight. No? Fine. You'll hear from me when I return to the League." And with that last word, Jakka turned and started walking directly toward Wren. Jakka stared into the bushes again, right where Wren was hiding, but he did not stop, giving no indication that Wren had been spotted. Jakka simply continued to make his way through the forest.

"The Dark Lord is apprehensive about the boy," Wren heard the Shadow Knight leader say. "Yet Jakka does not seem concerned."

"Perhaps he did not want to reveal anything to us about the boy?" one of the other Shadow Knights suggested.

"Yes, you may be right. I will not rue the day we can finally rid ourselves of that pompous ass. One day, I will slice that pretty little head off of his body and hold it for all the world to see." The other Shadow Knights laughed and cheered their leader on. "Gather the horses, we ride back for the Shadow Kingdom tonight."

***

Wren's head bounced off of Ragnvar's back with each steady gallop of his mighty stallion. He stole quick glances over at Jakka, but not once did Jakka look back. The four of them rode swiftly back through the night, and the only thing that kept Wren from falling asleep was the cold mist of the raging river. It was a clear, cool night and the stars speckled the night sky above them. Svela broke the silence.

"Viper, we are being followed, in the shallow cover of the forest on the other side of the river."

Ragnvar looked out into the night. "Can you see who they are?"

"They are dressed in dark cloaks, and they ride swift, black horses, not unlike your own."

"Shadow Knights," Ragnvar said calmly and Svela nodded her head in agreement.

"Let them be over there, the river divides us and their tactic of stealth tells me they won't bring any attention to themselves," Jakka interjected.

"You may be right, Jackal," Ragnvar said. "Still, I better inform the Elder when we return to the League. The Shadow is spreading further and faster than we anticipated."

"Let them come, I'll welcome them with my blade and my cock," Jakka laughed.

"Must you be so vile?" Svela snarled, though she kept her eyes fixed upon the forest.

"Have you fallen asleep, young Wren?" Ragnvar whispered over his shoulder.

"No, Sir Ragnvar, I am still awake," Wren replied.

"You have not uttered a word since we left the camp. I hope these battles have not scarred you too deeply."

"It is not the battle that frightens me, Sir Ragnvar," Wren said, a worried tremor filling his voice.

"What do you mean by that, Wren?"

"What are you two girls gossiping about over there?" Jakka chimed in.

Wren looked back, and this time Jakka looked him dead in his eye and held his gaze.

"They seem to have dropped back, I don't see any movement anymore," Svela reported.

"That won't be the last time we are followed," Ragnvar announced ominously.

***

The moon was full and large and ghostly and it produced shadows that danced wildly in the night. Wren drifted in and out of sleep as the rhythmic sounds of the horses' hooves pounded the earth beneath them. They rode through the night and well into the early hours of the morning. Wren finally felt relief when the large stone walls of the League peeked over the tops of the Northern Fir trees that lined the base of the White Lions Mountains. He was exhausted and he could barely even get down from Ragnvar's horse.

"Wren, I think we need to continue that conversation we were having earlier," Ragnvar said to him.

Wren nodded. "Whenever it is convenient to you Sir Ragnvar."

"I will need to inform the Elder of the ambush that transpired during the mission. You look like you could use some rest. Let us speak when you wake."

"Svela and Jakka, I request your presence in the Elder's Chambers for a mission debriefing."

"Can it not wait until the evening?" Jakka groaned.

"Unfortunately not, the Shadow is spreading, Jakka, we need to make preparations," Ragnvar replied.

"I am glad to see you all return safely." The Elder had emerged from the League on his own.

"My Lord," Wren said, bowing down to one knee.

"We have urgent matters to discuss, my Lord," Ragnvar spoke quickly.

The Elder's face was grave. "Viper, that will have to wait. I know you all just returned, but the League was handed an anonymous mission while you were gone."

"Anonymous, to us? Seems suspicious," Svela remarked.

"I feel a little unsettled myself, My Lord," Ragnvar added. "How could it have been anonymous?"

The Elder shook his head. "It appeared suddenly in my Chambers yesterday. A scroll, with no signature and no official stamp and no messenger."

"It matters not to me," Jakka said. "Let us carry it out, I was already getting bored again here." He chuckled to himself.

"I have not yet decided if we are to carry this mission out. Not only is its validity in question, but the target undermines the basic tenets of this League."

"What? It can't be." Wren had never seen Ragnvar like this.

"What is it, Father?" Svela demanded.

The Elder sighed. "The order is for us to carry out a direct assassination of the Shadow King himself."

Wren watched the color drain from Jakka's face.

Svela spoke first, "My Lord, how would we even undertake such an endeavor?"

The Elder remained silent, his face was somber.

"The perils of even reaching the Shadow Kingdom are near impossible to overcome. Even if we took a full team of support; that would render the League defenseless against an attack," Ragnvar reasoned.

"I have taken all of this under careful consideration, Sir Ragnvar. I waited for you all to return before making a decision on the matter."

Jakka still said nothing. Wren watched him carefully out of the side of his eye.

"Father, I spoke out earlier about the Shadow King, and what he represents. Taking this mission on would mean nearly certain death for us," Svela spoke quickly.

"I am entirely aware, my dear. I would like to discuss further with Sir Ragnvar about the anonymity of the letter. There may be some clues that we are not yet aware of. Svela, Jakka, you are more than welcome to join us."

"I, I am feeling a bit fatigued now, the big bastard almost flattened me with his warhammer back in the forest. I am afraid I will require a good night's rest before I'm ready to continue," Jakka said.

"Of course, Svela and Wren, why don't you do the same. I will fill the two of you in on everything after I discuss with the Elder."

The Jackal

Jakka walked briskly back inside and headed straight for his room. He threw his tunic off and put on his familiar League robes, and placed his curved longsword in the corner. He sat on the edge of his bed and ran his fingers back through his hair and exhaled. With slow deliberate movements, he went to close the door and popped open the window on the far wall of the room. He lifted himself up onto the sill, and reached around outside until he found a small ledge beneath the window where his large hand came upon an old rough sack which he brought back into the room. Carefully, Jakka unraveled the knot at the top and he opened it up. From it, he pulled out a scroll, nearly identical to the one that the Elder read from earlier. His hands shook and he undid the black wax that sealed it.

Jakka, the Plan is in motion. The decoy has been sent and it is now time for you to deliver on your promises. Remember our deal, and remember what awaits you when you succeed.

"No, it can't be." His voice quivered as he fell to his knees and held his face in his hands, letting out a cry.

The Betrayal

Wren heard Jakka wail from his room and it chilled him to his core, what could possibly make Jakka feel that way. He was already wary of Jakka, especially after the exchange he witnessed in the forest with the Shadow Knights. Wren lay down in his bed and pulled his blanket over his head. He listened quietly, and heard Jakka muttering to himself as he paced back and forth in his room frantically.

"What could he be doing?" Wren whispered to himself. He heard the door to Jakka's room open and then close. Wren jumped out of bed and followed the sound of Jakka's silent footsteps, he gripped the handle of his dagger tightly. He hid in the darkness and waited to see where Jakka was going. Down the cold, dark hallways, Wren stepped carefully so as not to make a noise. He watched as Jakka stopped outside of Svela's room and opened the door.

"Jakka? What are you doing?" Wren heard Svela ask sleepily.

But Jakka did not say a word. Wren felt chills run up and down his spine when in the faint flame of a torch on the wall, he saw tears streaming down Jakka's face.

"Jakka, are you okay? What happened?" Svela asked, rousing from her slumber.

A few moments later, Jakka emerged from the room with Svela slung over his shoulder, motionless. Wren followed them outside. There was no time to go wake Sir Ragnvar or call the Elder. He drew his dagger and revealed himself.

"Jakka! Stop right now, what are you doing?"

"Go away, Wren."

"Put Svela down! What have you done?"

"Trust me, boy, leave right now. I will not hold back!" Jakka threatened.

"Put her down Jakka!"

Jakka slung Svela over the back of his horse and turned back to Wren.

"Forget you saw this Wren, go back inside!"

"No! Let her go!" And Wren charged at Jakka but before Wren even got near Jakka, he saw him pull a black orb of pulsating energy out from under his robes.

"You asked for this, you little shit." He raised his hands and threw the energy at Wren, sending him backwards and knocking the wind from him.

Jakka laughed as a shadowy black cloud fell over his eyes, then turned back to his horse, mounted it and rode off with Svela toward the Shadow Kingdom. All Wren could remember was the fading sounds of the horse's hooves as he lost consciousness and drifted into darkness.

TO BE CONTINUED...

Be the first to review League of Assassins by clicking here.

League of Assassins Book 2
Preview

Wren

The long, winding road was still familiar to Wren even though it was now caked with a thick, sticky mud from all of the years of constant rainfall. Wren plodded along, making his way up the road, more than once he almost lost a boot as each step he took sank his foot down deep past his ankles. It was an eerie scene that he walked through, despite the rain, the trees were old and decayed with not a drop of green to be seen. The sky itself was perpetually gray here and what were once rolling hills of lively, luscious grass was scorched and the black wood rotted with death. Wren raised his hooded head and strained his eyes through the drops of rain that pelted his face. Over the tops of the barren trees, he could see tall plumes of ebony flames reaching toward the sky from the top of his village.

Further along, Wren spotted a pair of travelers up ahead. One was taller, a full grown man and the other a young boy, not far from his own age. Wren could hear them talking and as he approached them from behind, he recognized the younger one's voice as Tomas, a boy from the same village as him.

"Father", Tomas said from beneath his hood, "what are those black flames up ahead?"

"The shadow is upon us Tomas, we must hurry and save the others. Come along now."

Tomas and his father picked up their pace as Wren followed closely. The faster they hurried, the deeper into the mud their feet sank. Wren watched as Tomas slipped and fell to one knee, letting out a yelp. He looked back in Wren's direction, but did not acknowledge that Wren was standing not ten yards from him. In fact, he seemed to look right through him and off into the distance.

"Tomas, are you alright?" Wren asked, but Tomas did not answer.

"Father, what is that down there?" Tomas pointed back down the road from which they came. Wren turned to look as well and saw what Tomas was referring to. Racing up the road at full speed was a large black figure riding an even blacker horse. His cape flew back in the wind and it howled behind him like a banshee. The figure was closing in on Tomas, and Wren watched as he stood up tall in his stirrups and pulled a long Ebony Blade from behind his back.

"Tomas, run!" the father yelled.

Tomas tried in vain to run, but the mud was too thick and he indeed lost one of his boots. The horse and rider gained quickly, Wren could feel the ground shaking as each hoof pounded into the packed dirt, even as wet as it was, it sounded like thunder itself was rolling toward them. The figure raised his blade high in the air and brought it down with all his fury, decapitating Tomas instantly. Blood splattered everywhere, spraying even across the horse's face, but the mighty beast kept running up the road toward Tomas' father.

"Tomas!" The father fell to his knees and wept. "You bastard! Come down here and fight me like a man!" The horse stopped, and the black figure stepped down onto the ground. Even off of his steed, he was imposing, his Ebony Armor glistened from the rain and his long blade stood taller than most regular-sized men. Wren watched as Tomas' father drew a dulled sword from his belt, and even from where Wren was, he could see that it was chipped and made of an inferior alloy. Even so, the father charged at the man and swung his sword, but the Shadow Knight sidestepped him with ease, turning and kicking the father down into the mud. The man spat mud out of his mouth, and ignored that which was plastered to his face. He dropped his sword and, to Wren's surprise, he started to laugh.

"You think you are some kind of hero for your little Shadow King?" The father blurted out between laughs.

The tall Shadow Knight stood there, and watched the father as he tried to get back to his feet.

"Do you actually think that we're afraid of you lot? Killing women and children, men who have never swung a sword or donned a piece of armor."

A silence grew between the two as Wren watched on. The Shadow Knight placed his Ebony Blade back into its sheath and began to get back onto his horse.

"You fucking coward!" the father yelled after the silence, and his laughter turned to sobs.

The Shadow Knight reared his massive steed and thick, black smoke shot out of the nostrils of the great beast.

"Where do you think you're going? Kill me!" he spat in the direction of the Shadow Knight as he rode by. The Shadow Knight continued a few yards away but then turned back and faced the hysterical man.

"Alright, bastard, let's see what you've got—" Before the father could even finish his sentence, the Shadow Knight impaled him with a black blade of raw and boiling energy, it crackled and spat with dark light as the father's skin blackened and was torn asunder. He held the father's corpse high in the air, as blood poured out in rivulets harder than the falling rain. With a flick of his sword, the body hit the ground with a wet thud, not far from the resting spot of his son's head. In silence, he stared directly at Wren for a moment, then he turned his horse and the Shadow Knight galloped off into the distance, toward the shadowy fires that enveloped the town.

Ragnvar

Ragnvar paced back and forth on the cold, stone floors of the infirmary. His steps were hard and full of fury, and they echoed throughout the halls, and faded down the distant corridors like the last fleeting moment of a distant memory. He paused and turned toward the door as he sensed a presence.

"Any improvement?" the Elder asked, as he entered the room.

"None, my Lord," Ragnvar answered gravely.

The Elder walked past Ragnvar and circled the bed where Wren lay. He gently brushed the hair out of Wren's face and looked back up at Ragnvar.

"Do not carry this with you, Sir Ragnvar. There is nothing that any of us could have done."

"All the signs were there, my Lord. The boy even wanted to tell me something, but I never gave him the chance."

"At the moment, there were more pressing matters that we needed to attend to."

Ragnvar continued to pace the floor as the Elder watched him, a curious smile began to form across his aging face.

"You are concerned, not only for Jakka and Svela, but for Wren as well."

Ragnvar stopped.

"My Lord, I am concerned that the sanctity of our Guild has been compromised. Something happened on this night, something sinister and foul. At this moment, it seems only the boy knows anything about it, so I will continue to wait until he wakes so that he can tell me what he intended to say."

"And if he never awakes?" the Elder replied calmly.

Ragnvar remained silent for a moment, grimacing, before he finally spoke. "How is his wound?"

The Elder drew back the throw that covered Wren and revealed a long, deep wound as black as scorched earth that spanned nearly six inches long and festered with infection.

"The medicine is not taking as of now and the infection will continue to spread throughout his body."

"What other course is there to take?" Ragnvar asked.

The Elder paused before he answered. "I have already gone ahead and sent for Verigo, he may be our only hope."

"Verigo? The barber surgeon?"

The Elder nodded. "Yes, he should be arriving imminently. I fear the situation is much graver than you may think, Sir Ragnvar."

"I do not welcome the thought of inviting such a treacherous guest into our Guild," Ragnvar said quietly, without looking up.

"He is our last hope," the Elder replied, raising his voice ever so slightly.

"Very well, I shall stay in here with the boy while Verigo performs his treatment."

The Elder's face softened, and Ragnvar watched as the blood slowly drained from the scar that gashed across it.

"I would expect no less from you, Sir Ragnvar."

"My Lord, I fear the worst about—"

The Elder interrupted before Ragnvar could finish, "I know, Sir Ragnvar. She is my daughter, do not underestimate the grief that is consuming me."

"I will make this Guild whole again. Jakka must pay."

"Oh? You are so hasty to lay guilt on Jakka, when we are uncertain of what has transpired."

"My Lord?"

"Sometimes when we believe we are most certain, that is when we lose our clarity."

A squire entered the infirmary, leaving behind him a frail, crooked man with thinning black hair and dry, pasty skin. He wore black robes that dragged behind him as he walked and he carried an old leather apothecary case that was faded and worn from years of use.

"Welcome, Verigo, we appreciate your haste in this time of crisis." The Elder walked over to shake the barber's hand.

"Always a pleasure to help out those of us on the fringes of the world." A sly smile crept over Verigo's face as he looked over at Ragnvar.

"Sir Ragnvar, it has been a while since our paths have crossed. I hope you are finding yourself in good health." Verigo held out his hand.

Sir Ragnvar looked down at the thin, pallid hand and ignored it. "Get to work, barber, we don't have much time to spare here."

"Still as charming as ever I see," Verigo said, as Ragnvar walked past him and over to Wren.

Ragnvar pulled back the throw to show him Wren's wound. Verigo's eyes opened wide, as he moved in for a closer look.

"Oh my, what darkness has this young boy stumbled across?"

"Do you recognize the infection?" Ragnvar asked.

"I know it all too well."

"Can you cure it?"

"If we're lucky. I will have to drain his blood tonight and clean it, before we can even begin to treat the infection."

The Elder nodded thoughtfully. "Sir Ragnvar will stay in the room tonight, feel free to employ his help if you need it."

Verigo nodded and set his bag down on the floor.

"I'll need a basin to drain the boy's blood into, preferably something clean."

Ragnvar ignored the barber surgeon, and continued to pace the floor.

"Am I speaking too softly for you, Sir Ragnvar?"

"I am not your nurse, barber. Do I look like I have a set of tits for you to order around?"

"Now, now, aren't we touchy? I thought you cared for the young man."

"I care about the security of the Guild and the realm, and the boy has information that could prove to be very useful."

Wren coughed violently and blood like black ichor spewed from his mouth.

"Well if you ever want him to tell you that information, I would go find a basin... quickly." Verigo retrieved a cloth from his bag and wiped Wren's mouth.

Ragnvar glared at Verigo, who was already focused on preparing his patient; reluctantly, he rose to accommodate the barber. He came across one of the squires in the Great Hall, the one that brought Verigo into the infirmary.

"You there, squire. Any idea where I can find a clean basin?"

"There are some out in the stables, where the horses feed and water from."

"Are they clean? It is for a medical procedure for Wren."

"Yes, I wash them myself every week."

"Very well, thank you for your help."

"Sir Ragnvar?"

"Yes, squire?"

"How... how is Wren doing? He is my friend from when we were squires together."

Ragnvar looked at the young squire and sighed. "You needn't concern yourself with such information, squire. He is alive, that is all I will disclose for now."

"Wren is tougher than you know, Sir Ragnvar. He will survive this, I know he will." The squire smiled. "Come, I will show you to the stables to find a basin."

***

Outside, the evening was cool and clear. A calm stillness fell over the Guild, quieter than most. Ragnvar felt something was off, and the squire's sudden panic confirmed Ragnvar's uneasiness.

"The horses, they are gone!" the squire screamed, panicking as he moved quickly between the stables.

"What do you mean? How can this be?" Sir Ragnvar yelled.

"I... I don't know. It seems like someone has released them. Who would do such a thing?"

"Jakka," Sir Ragnvar growled under his breath.

"Sir Ragnvar?"

Ragnvar grabbed a basin from the squire and turned to run back to the Guild.

When he returned to the infirmary, the Elder was back speaking with Verigo. Over the barber's shoulder, the Elder flashed Ragnvar a grave look.

"Ah, perfect!" Verigo said, "We'll make a nurse out of you yet, Sir Ragnvar."

The barber took the basin and set it at the foot of Wren's bed. Ragnvar looked at the young boy and grimaced at the wound. Wren's survival seemed less and less optimistic with each fleeting moment.

"If one of you would come assist me," Verigo said, as he readied Wren's arm.

Ragnvar went over and took the small arm in his hands. It was cold and fragile to the touch.

"Hold on tightly, Sir, this may cause him to flinch a bit, even in his unconscious state."

Verigo produced a long thin blade that he carefully cleaned before sliding it down Wren's arm, slicing it wide open along one of the main arteries. Thick, dark crimson blood started to flow heavily out of the arm and down into the basin.

"It is darker than I imagined it to be," the Elder remarked.

The color started to drain from Wren as his life-force emptied out before Ragnvar's eyes. They stood for what seemed like hours, until every last drop was sapped from Wren's body. The metallic stench filled the air.

"Now what?" Ragnvar asked impatiently.

"Now I clean the blood with fire and treat the wound, while the infection is still fresh I will apply a salve and hope that it takes. If not, I'm sorry to say the young boy will have no chance to survive this."

"What sort of salve is this, Verigo?"

"It consists of a paste of ground-up tobakk leaves and malort root. It is an old alchemist recipe that I usually apply to wounds like this."

"Do you get much work with wounds like this?" the Elder asked.

"Not many, my Lord. I recently did some bloodletting work, but nothing substantial for wound salves. That is why I did not bring any malort root with me today, I'll have to go forage for some."

"Perhaps, Sir Ragnvar, you could go collect some malort root while Verigo gets to work on young Wren's blood."

"If I may suggest sending one of the squires, my Lord," Ragnvar said.

"Sir Ragnvar, I trust more in your tracker's eye when it comes to these things. If I may request you to undertake this task, I would feel better about it."

The Elder gave a slight nod to Ragnvar.

"Of course, my Lord. I shall go immediately."

"And Verigo, I must retire back to my chambers momentarily, please forgive me in my age, I shall return to assist as soon as I am able."

"Take your time, my Lord," Verigo replied. "The burning of the blood will take longer than one would think."

"Very well, I leave Wren in your very capable hands, Verigo."

***

"Sir Ragnvar, come with me," the Elder said when they were clear of the infirmary.

"Yes, my Lord, is everything alright?"

"I fear that this situation is darker than I first believed," the Elder whispered.

"I'm afraid I don't follow, my Lord. Do you speak of Wren's health?"

"No, head to the woods behind the stables. There is plenty of malort root there to harvest. Wait there, and make sure you are not followed."

"My Lord?" Ragnvar asked, confused.

"Go, Sir Ragnvar. And wait, until you see it. The situation has just turned urgent, and I fear we are all in grave danger, especially Svela."

"See what, my Lord?"

"When you see it, you will know."

Thank You From Story Ninjas

Story Ninjas Publishing would like to thank you for reading this product. We hope you found value in our book and would love to hear your feedback. Please provide your constructive criticism in a review on Amazon. Also, feel free to share this book with your friends through various social media platforms.

Other Books by Story Ninjas

Story Ninjas Publishing hopes you enjoyed this book. You can find more of our products, by checking out our Amazon page.

About Story Ninjas

Story Ninjas Publishing is an independent book publisher. Our stories range from science fiction to paranormal romance. Our goal is to create stories that are not only entertaining but endearing. We believe engaging narrative can lead to personal growth. Through unforgettable characters and a powerful plot, we portray themes that are relevant to today's issues. Our hope is that readers find lessons they can apply to their everyday lives so that the stories live on through the actions of each person they touch. Additionally, we provide creative non-fiction books that are meant to serve as tools to help people solve everyday problems. We hope you find our products entertaining and helpful.

You can find more Story Ninja's products on Amazon.com.

Follow Story Ninjas!!!
Website: www.Story-Ninjas.com
Email: Story-Ninjas@Story-Ninjas.com
Instagram: @StoryNinjas
Facebook: StoryNinjasHQ
LinkedIn: Story-Ninjas

Blogger: Story-NinjasHQ
Twitter: @StoryNinjas
Youtube: @StoryNinjas
Amazon: Story Ninjas
Podcast: Polymathics

Made in the USA
Las Vegas, NV
04 January 2021